Badger Publishing Limited, Oldmedow Road, Hardwick Industrial Estate, King's Lynn PE30 4JJ
Telephone: 01438 791037

www.badgerlearning.co.uk

DEATH ROAD

JON MAYHEW

Death Road ISBN 978-1-78147-969-8

Text © Jon Mayhew 2014
Complete work © Badger Publishing Limited 2014

Publisher: Susan Ross
Senior Editor: Danny Pearson
Publishing Assistant: Claire Morgan
Copyeditor: Cheryl Lanyon
Designer: Bigtop Design Ltd

2 4 6 8 10 9 7 5 3 1

In the year 2320 the Great Disaster happened.

A nuclear war destroyed all the main towns and cities of the world.

The water dried up and the world became one big desert.

Then a plague came. It turned ordinary people into flesh-hungry zombies.

The unaffected survivors built walls around what was left of their cities to keep the zombies out.

This is the world Omak lives in.

CHAPTER 1

Omak sat in the driver's seat of the Blood Bug, his small, armoured car. He revved the engine and drove straight at the car in front of him. The street and buildings flashed by. He could see the tough, iron plate that covered the other car's front. It was so close that he could even see the scratches that scarred its blue paintwork and the loose rivets that rattled as it bounced towards him.

"Silva Dacosta," Omak muttered. "You're not getting this job."

The screaming engine noise filled the car as it flew towards Silva's car. Silva wasn't chickening out either. One of them would have to brake or they would smash into each other.

Omak could see Silva's wide eyes, her short, spiky white hair through the tiny windscreen. If he didn't brake now, that would be it!

He dragged the steering wheel to the left and felt the rear end of the car drift. The whole Blood Bug rattled along as it turned into a skid. Sparks flashed from the front wing as it clipped Silva's car. Omak swung the steering back and managed to straighten out. The seat belt gripped his chest and shoulders as he slammed on the brakes and came to a squealing stop.

Omak nearly head-butted the dashboard of his car as he stopped. He looked out to see Silva's buggy, Blue Flash, half on the road half on the path, its rear tyres smoking. He jumped out. Silva was climbing out of her car too.

"Are you mad?" she yelled, her cheeks red with anger. She was small, like Omak. They had to be to drive the cramped armoured buggies they used to deliver things to the cities. Petrol was expensive and drivers had to be light. The smaller you were, the more things you could carry in the car. Kids were the best drivers.

"Me?" Omak shouted, slapping his chest. "Why didn't you brake sooner? I nearly killed you!"

"Ha! Your heap of scrap couldn't do my Blue Flash any harm!" Silva sneered.

"Then what are you grumbling about?" Omak said, grinning. "Are you trying to get my attention?"

Silva clenched her fists. "As if! What are you doing here?" she asked through gritted teeth.

"Same as you, I guess," Omak said, looking up at the tower block they stood outside. "I've got an appointment with the Mayor."

"Oh no you don't," Silva said, staring at Omak.

Omak and Silva did the same job. They were Posties. They drove their small armoured buggies between the cities, delivering mail, parcels, pets, messages, food, anything as long as people paid them. Fuel was scarce but the cars ran on all kinds of things; petrol was best but old cooking oil would do if necessary.

"Look, Silva…" Omak stammered, "I really need this job…"

"You can't do it," Silva said, fixing Omak with her emerald eyes.

"Yeah? Says who?" Omak grinned. He didn't feel very happy, though. He needed money badly. Mum owed money to the water seller, the food man, and worst of all she owed rent to the Council itself. If Omak didn't get this job then Mum would have to work as a slave in the sewers until she'd paid off the debt. That's how it worked in this city. And there were plenty of

Posties, young kids eager to risk the outside world to deliver. Silva and Omak were the best and found themselves fighting each other for work all the time.

"I do," Silva snapped. "You mustn't do this job, Omak!"

"I've got to. Anyway, you're only saying that 'cos you want it," Omak said. He didn't know why Silva was a Postie. She was rich compared to him. Sometimes he really fancied her, but what would a rich girl like her see in a deadbeat like him? He had to think fast. "I think I'll have the last laugh," he said staring over her shoulder at her car. "You left your handbrake off. Blue Flash is rolling away!"

Silva gave a yelp and turned around.

Omak ran up the steps of the Mayor's building, swinging open the glass doors. They were double doors with two handles in the middle. Omak

pulled off his dust scarf and tied it around the
handles, locking the doors. Silva slammed herself
against the glass.

"Omak, come back!" Silva yelled. "Don't take
that job!"

A huge security guard came out from behind his
desk and frowned at Omak.

"Quickly," Omak panted. "That girl is mad. I
think she has Snapper fever!"

The guard's eyes widened and he pulled out a
Taser. "I'll deal with her son," he said, taking a
step forwards. Snappers were the living dead who
roamed the desert lands between cities. One bite
from a Snapper was enough to infect you with
a fever that drove you insane. Snappers usually
gave you more than one bite, though.

Omak grinned at the look of alarm on Silva's
face. She'd guessed what Omak had said to the
guard and quickly backed down the steps. Omak

ran up the stairs that stood at the side of the
disused lifts.

"That's the competition put out of the game," he
laughed, jumping the steps two at a time towards
the Mayor's office. "The job is mine!"

CHAPTER 2

The Snappers looked close. Omak could see their yellow teeth and their grey skin. They reached out with long, black fingernails. Desert dust blew up around them as they stumbled along searching for meat. ANY meat.

Once the Snappers had been human just like Omak, but after the Great Disaster they changed. They never died. They never slept. They just wandered in the hot, waterless land that surrounded the walled city of Birmingham. Mindless and hungry.

Omak shivered and put down the telescope he had been looking through.

"I bet you're glad to be up here in my office," Mayor Blanchard said behind him. "You wouldn't want to be down there with those monsters."

"I'm glad I'm safe behind the walls of the city," replied Omak, shaking himself.

Mayor Blanchard laughed and took a sip from his glass. Omak heard ice cubes clink and stared. How could the Mayor get ice? Water was in such short supply. Everything was in short supply: food, clothing, light, shade, space. The Great Disaster had swept civilisation away and the survivors had built walls around their cities to keep the Snappers, and other things, out.

"Mmm, there's nothing like an iced drink," Mayor Blanchard said, raising his glass. He took another sip, smacking his thick lips and belching. "You want some?"

Omak nodded slowly and the Mayor heaved himself off his big, black chair and waddled over to a table that held an ice bucket and some bottles of water.

"How's your mother?" the Mayor asked, pouring a drink.

Omak licked his parched lips as the ice chunks clunked into the glass.

"F-fine," he stammered. "She's fine."

"Fine?" Mayor Blanchard said, staring out of the window at the crumbling city below. "How can any of us be fine in this hell hole?"

"I don't know," Omak said. He didn't really understand.

"How old arc you, Omak? Sixteen? Seventeen?"

"Something like that, I guess," Omak said, with a shrug.

"You won't really remember the world before the Great Disaster," the Mayor said with a sigh. "Life was easy then. If only we'd known it."

"Right," said Omak.

"Sometimes I wish we'd all died back then," Mayor Blanchard said, still staring out of the window. He turned. "Instead of living like this. There are too many mouths, Omak. Not enough food."

"If you say so," Omak muttered. All he was interested in was his next job so he could keep Mum out of debt and his car rolling.

The Mayor clapped his hands.

"Well, this is a big job, Omak," he said. He passed the drink. "Very important. Lives depend on it."

"What do you want me to deliver?" asked Omak.

Mayor Blanchard walked over to a small, white fridge. Omak had noticed it when he first came in. Fridges were expensive. They used too much electricity. The Mayor opened the fridge door and took out a small, glass test tube.

"This," he said. "It's the cure for the Snapper fever that has broken out in London. People are dying. This is their only hope."

"But can a little bottle like that treat the whole of London?" Omak stared at the tiny test tube.

"It only takes a microscopic droplet of this stuff to cure hundreds, maybe thousands, of people, Omak," the Mayor said, holding the antidote up.

"That's an important mission," Omak agreed. His heart thudded. He'd taken all kinds of things to London before, valuable things, machine parts, electronics, and documents. But he'd never taken anything so precious. "How come you didn't choose Silva? Her car is faster than mine and she takes passengers. You could send a doctor…"

Mayor Blanchard narrowed his eyes and pursed his lips.

"Silva asks too many questions, Omak," the Mayor said. He looked tired. "And I don't trust her. Complete this mission and you'll be a hero. You'll never have to work again. Your mother's debts will be cleared. I promise."

Omak frowned. "Why can't London make their own medicine?"

"They can, but they've run out and it'll take them six months to make more," explained the Mayor. "They don't have six months. We're the nearest supply. So we're giving them ours. The Snapper fever is spreading like wildfire." He slipped the test tube into a metal flask and passed it to Omak. "We're depending on you."

"Don't worry," Omak said, taking the flask and slipping it into his rucksack. "The cure will be in London by midnight tonight."

There was no sign of Silva when Omak came out of the Mayor's office. He jumped into the Blood Bug and headed for the garage.

The streets of Birmingham were full of people going to their daily work. Omak tried to imagine what it had been like before the Great Disaster. There would have been more cars, he knew that. The cars would have been bigger than his machine, which only held one and was like a high-speed box made of plate steel. Now, most people walked or got the few electric buses that still rattled around the city streets. Mum had told him that it used to rain a lot. Omak found this hard to imagine. He remembered a rainstorm from when he was a toddler. Water had fallen from the sky and he remembered the feel of it on his face. That was years ago and it hadn't rained since. Sometimes Omak heard thunder out across the desert plains to the north and east.

Most of the buildings in the city had collapsed or burned down in the Great Disaster. People had repaired some of them as best they could and, as the years rolled on and the climate grew hotter, houses made of mud brick and old wood had sprung up in-between the older buildings.

The huge gates of the city loomed before him and slowly swung open. Omak felt a shiver of excitement as he drove out into the desert towards danger.

CHAPTER 3

Once, Omak's Mum told him, there had been huge roads called motorways that joined all the cities together. Thousands of cars rumbled up and down them every day at speeds of up to eighty miles an hour. Omak wished the motorways still existed as he bounced and rattled over the rocky ground.

Posties tended to drive in as straight a line as possible, to make their journeys quicker. This meant that tracks had formed over the years, but they were rough and full of holes and stones.

The Blood Bug had powerful suspension but the journey rattled his teeth. He looked ahead across the flat horizon. Not a building in sight. Here and there, little clouds of dust billowed up where another Postie was speeding off on a mission. Maybe to Bristol or one of the smaller settlements in the east like Cambridge or Lincoln. Other clouds of dust moved more slowly.

Snappers, Omak thought. *Huge swarms of them.*

Sometimes, if the Snappers were drawn to something big, they ended up in large swarms. These were dangerous because the sheer weight of the bodies would stop a buggy in its tracks and although the Snappers couldn't get in, the driver couldn't get out either. Omak had come across the wrecks of a few buggies. The drivers had gone mad and climbed out, or suffocated in their cars. Snapper swarms were best avoided.

A sudden thud from behind him shook Omak from his thoughts. Something had just rammed him! He glanced in the mirror.

"Silva!" he hissed, glimpsing Blue Flash through the dirt kicked up by his rear wheels.

Blue Flash appeared out of the dust storm again. Silva had a ramming plate which made her buggy look like a mini bulldozer.

Omak dragged his wheel left and Silva flashed past him. He just saw her wide eyes and gritted teeth. The Blood Bug began to drift and he wrestled with the steering to get it straight. Silva was in front of him now and blocked each attempt he made to get past. Then she slammed her brakes on.

Omak jammed his foot on the brake and tried to turn sharp right. The buggy clipped the rear of Silva's car and shot off the rough track.

Omak clenched his teeth and clung onto the wheel as he bounced and skipped across the uneven ground that lay either side of the road. He winced and groaned as he heard rocks smack against the underside of his car. If he didn't slow down, he'd rip the bottom out of the Blood Bug.

A wall of dust hid the outside world. Omak eased his foot off the gas and screeched to a halt. Gradually, the dirt began to settle and the world became clear again. Omak stared out but couldn't see any sign of Silva.

"What is she playing at?" he muttered to himself.

Slowly, he rolled back onto the track. A slight grating sound made him uneasy but he couldn't worry about that now. He had to get the cure for the Snapper fever to London.

The engines of the buggy roared into life as Omak speeded up. His hands shook. Why had Silva rammed him like that? What was she trying to do? Kill him? Posties were competitive and ribbed each other about their cars, he'd even seen the odd fist fight, but nobody tried to run you off the road.

His nerves calmed as he drove and Omak tried to distract himself from thinking about the attack. He stared across the horizon. He'd seen some old pictures of the green fields that once filled this land but he found it hard to believe that this had ever been anything but desert. Here and there a few cactus plants poked above the ground but mostly it was dead.

He came to a rock outcrop and his heart pounded. It sat at the side of the road in the distance like some kind of beast waiting to pounce. A perfect place for an ambush, he said to himself. He could imagine Silva parked at the other side of the huge rock, revving her engine and waiting to ram him side-on.

Omak smiled and revved the engine so she could hear him coming if she was there. Then he speeded up. He needed to be going at top speed if he was to avoid being rammed. The huge rock drew nearer and nearer. Just before he passed it, Omak punched a red button on his dashboard.

The Blood Bug doubled in speed, pressing Omak back into his seat as the turbo booster cut in. Omak caught a glimpse of blue. Looking back he saw Silva hurtling off across the desert at a right angle – he'd sped past her intercept. She was a good driver, though, and quickly had the car back under control. It bounced and skipped across the desert, heading straight towards Omak.

Omak speeded up until the engine screamed. He watched the fuel dropping and the temperature of the engine rising, but Silva was still on his tail.

I'm going to have to slow down, Omak thought. He could smell oil and rubber burning. If he carried on at this speed, the car would blow up or roll on the uneven road surface.

Blue Flash began to come alongside Omak. He could see Silva's angry expression, her narrow, determined eyes through her goggles. She crunched against the side of the Blood Bug, sending him veering off the road. Omak gripped the wheel and dragged it back on track, smashing against Blue Flash. This time Silva lost the road for a second, but then she came back crunching against his buggy again. Omak could feel the pressure of her car pushing him towards the edge of the track. He looked ahead and his eyes widened.

A thick knot of Snappers filled the road ahead. They hadn't noticed Omak or Silva hurtling towards them and were all leaning over something. Omak swallowed hard. It was probably a car crash or breakdown, and now they'd been trapped by Snappers.

Silva still pushed at the side of the Blood Bug. Omak steered off the road, taking Silva by surprise. The two of them veered left, bouncing and clattering across the rocky ground. But Silva was half on the road still and she crashed into the Snappers, sending bodies and limbs scattering everywhere.

Brown, sludgy blood sprayed across Omak's windscreen and he had to use some of his precious screen wash to clear it. The screen went dark as the blood smeared and clogged with dust, then it cleared and Omak saw the open road ahead of him.

Silva had shot away from the road and didn't look like stopping. Dead Snappers hung from her bonnet and he could tell she was having trouble controlling Blue Flash.

"Well it's your own fault, girl," Omak said, looking in the mirror. A few Snappers stumbled away from the swarm after her. Omak felt a twinge of guilt. He felt he should try and help her, but he had to deliver the cure. He couldn't afford to stop and, after all, she'd attacked him.

A terrible clanking noise came from the engine in the back of Omak's buggy and smoke filled the car. Omak coughed, tears stinging his eyes. He had to get out, the car was on fire. He slammed on the brakes and pulled on the door handle. The lid of the Blood Bug shot up and Omak staggered out gasping and choking. He snatched his breathing mask and put it on. The air outside was full of poisons. They didn't kill you straight away but after an hour or two you could suffocate out here.

He glanced up. Some of the Snappers had seen him stop and were turning away from the prey on the road. If he didn't put the fire out, the engine would explode. But the Snappers had caught his scent and were staggering towards him. In a matter of minutes he would be fighting for his life. And he was outnumbered.

CHAPTER 4

The Snappers staggered nearer. Omak could see their blistered, grey skin and the dry, wispy hair that hung around their skeleton faces. He could smell the smoke billowing from the back of his car, too.

Ignoring the Snappers who inched closer, Omak leaped back to the car and wrenched a fire extinguisher from under his seat. Then he pulled a lever that popped open the rear engine compartment.

Small flames flickered into view as the lid lifted. Omak pointed the extinguisher into the engine and blasted it with white foam. The engine hissed and Omak heard something crack as it cooled rapidly. More smoke boiled out of the car but the flames were gone.

A foot scuffed the stones on the ground and Omak spun round to see the first of the Snappers about to reach him. Without stopping, Omak brought the empty fire extinguisher down heavily onto the Snapper's skull.

The zombie had been out in the sun for a long time. It was dry and scorched. Its head caved in like an eggshell. There was no real blood, just the brown sludge of what was left of the creature's brain.

More Snappers followed. Omak hurled the metal extinguisher, knocking the head from another Snapper's shoulders. *These are old creatures, weak and fragile,* he thought, hopefully.

All Posties carried some kind of anti-Snapper weapon and Omak had two. One was a small pistol and the other was a baseball bat that sat next to the fire extinguisher under his seat. The pistol was useful close up but the bat cleared a space around Omak so that there was less chance of being bitten. Omak ran round the car, dodging the grasping hands of the Snappers. He grabbed the bat from its place and swung it round, cracking the skull of the third zombie.

More had crept around the car. Omak was glad he had his breathing mask on. He'd smelled Snappers before. They stank and they looked horrible so close. He knew that they'd once been ordinary people like him, but the fever had dried their brains out and made them almost immortal with an eternal hunger for flesh.

Omak swung again, knocking down two of the Snappers this time. He jabbed the bat at another and then clambered onto the roof of his buggy. More Snappers were wandering over towards him now. They crowded around the car, grabbing at his legs as he smacked them away with the bat.

He could see the burned-out shell of a Postie's buggy on the road. That's what they had been so interested in before Omak and Silva interrupted them. Omak shivered. There wasn't much left of whoever was in there. They must have broken down just like Omak.

A horrible thought struck him. Did Silva attack that Postie too? Was she somehow helping the Snappers by feeding Posties to them?

All this went through Omak's mind as he swung the baseball bat back and forth at the mob around the car.

"Get away from me, you filthy Snappers!" he yelled, kicking at them and swinging his bat. More fell but more seemed to appear. He could see a dust cloud in the distance and his heart sank. *Another swarm of them,* he thought.

A large Snapper, younger and less sun-bleached than the rest, grabbed Omak's ankle and tried to pull him down. Omak cursed as he slipped on the smooth roof of the car. He fell onto his bottom as he swung the bat down on the creature's arm. A horrible snapping sound filled the air as the Snapper's grip loosened. Omak followed up with a sideways swing and was rewarded with the sound of the creature's skull cracking.

Sweat stung Omak's eyes and the sun blazed down on him. He gasped for breath as he swung the bat across the heads of the Snappers. He was getting weaker by the second. He needed water and shade. The dust cloud had grown larger now and Omak recognised the sound of engines. In the distance he saw Blue Flash appear. Had Silva come to watch him die?

The buggy came nearer, filling the air with the roar of its engine. Then its brakes screeched and it spun sidelong towards Omak and his car. The Snappers turned their heads to see what this new noise was.

Blue Flash skated sideways across the ground now, kicking up rocks and dust as it slid straight for Omak's car and the crowd of Snappers that surrounded it. The zombies weren't smart enough to get out of the way and Silva's car crunched into them, crushing them into the ground.

Then Blue Flash hit the Blood Bug with a sickening crunch of metal on metal. Omak fell forwards onto the roof of Silva's car. She revved the engine and with a squeal of tyres sped off away from the wreckage and dead Snappers. Omak gripped the parcel rack that covered the roof and gritted his teeth.

"You won't kill me that easily!" he yelled above the engine noise. He was glad that the breathing mask kept the sand and fumes out of his mouth and eyes.

Omak's arms ached with the effort of staying on the roof. Silva drove on, bouncing over dunes and rocks. She jumped a dry stream at one point. Omak tried not to be impressed but Silva could drive!

But Omak could barely hang on as Silva swerved all over the desert, avoiding old tree stumps or wreckage or rocks. His arms ached and his head thumped. He needed rest and water. Soon he would slide off the roof. Then he would be at the mercy of the Snappers or Silva's tyres.

He clung on to Blue Flash. The car took a sharp left turn and Omak felt his grip break. For a second he flew through the air, weightless, and then pain stabbed through his body as he rolled and tumbled across the ground. The last thing he heard was the sound of Silva's engine coming closer.

CHAPTER 5

Cool water wet Omak's lips and at first he thought he was in heaven. The blazing sun had gone and a beautiful pair of green eyes smiled down on him.

"Are you an angel?" he croaked.

"I'm afraid not, Omak," Silva said, grinning.

Omak awoke fully and lurched upright, knocking the cup of water from Silva's hand. "Where am I? What's going on? Why did you try to kill me?"

"Whoa! You're in a Safe Station," Silva said, easing him back. "And I didn't try to kill you. I saved your stupid life!"

Omak found he was lying on a small bed in a cool, shady room. The walls were concrete and plain. A small chest of drawers stood in the corner along with a table and some chairs. Safe Stations were small, concrete bunkers where Posties could hide out if they had broken down or needed food or water in an emergency. There were lots of them dotted along the route between Birmingham and London.

Omak scowled at Silva.

"So I'm not an angel anymore?" she teased. Omak felt his cheeks blaze.

"What do you mean you didn't try to kill me?" he snapped. "You tried to ram me off the road!"

"I wanted to stop you…"

"Stop me from saving the lives of everyone in London?" Omak yelled, thumping his fists into the mattress.

"No!" Silva shouted back. "I was trying to stop you from infecting everyone in London!"

"What are you talking about?" Omak asked.

"That so-called cure you were carrying was actually a very strong version of the Snapper fever," Silva explained. "If you'd taken that to London, everyone in the city would have become infected."

"How do you know all this?"

"A few months ago, Mayor Blanchard had me running letters back and forth to London," Silva explained. "Then I was carrying passengers from London to Birmingham. Friends of Blanchard's, and they weren't planning to go back to London."

"So?" Omak said. He didn't want to believe Silva. "It's a free country. People can live where they want."

"True, but these were powerful people, Omak. Why would they suddenly up and move to Birmingham?" Silva said. Omak shrugged. Silva sighed and carried on. "Well I got curious. When Blanchard sent more of these mails, I opened one and read it."

"You didn't!" Omak gasped. "That's the worst thing a Postie can do. You betrayed the trust of your client!"

"And a good job I did, too," Silva cut in. "The letter spelled out Blanchard's plan: to wipe out the population of London with the Snapper virus."

"But why?"

"London is a big city," Silva said. "Thousands of people. Blanchard thinks that if he wipes out a whole city then there'll be more food and supplies to go round. He thinks London is too big. It uses up too much food and water."

"That's horrible," Omak said, faintly. He remembered the Mayor's words when they'd met yesterday morning.

"Sometimes I wish we'd all died back then," Mayor Blanchard had said. "Instead of living like this. There are too many mouths, Omak. Not enough food."

"I couldn't let you get to London," Silva explained. "I tried to stop you yesterday but you pulled that trick and sent the ape with the Taser after me…"

"I just thought you were after my job," Omak muttered. His stomach tightened and he felt angry. "How could Blanchard do such a thing?"

Silva shrugged this time. "Who knows?" she said. "But if you'd handed that test tube over and they'd opened it, you'd have been one of the first to be infected. Or Blanchard would have had you killed on the way back."

"How long have I been out?" Omak groaned.

"You slept through the night," Silva said. "Blanchard will expect you to have delivered the virus by now."

Omak struggled up off the bed. "We need to get back to Birmingham," he muttered, wincing at the pain that shot through his body. "I want a word with Mayor Blanchard."

"We need to get your car back first," Silva said. "And then we need a plan."

*

Omak's car stood where they had left it. Most of the Snappers had moved on somewhere else overnight. A few stumbled around the car but Silva and Omak soon ran them over or finished them off with an axe that Silva was fond of using.

Now they stood looking at the car. Omak kicked the tyres. "She's not as bad as I expected," he said. "Still in one piece."

"The engine is badly fried," Silva said, slamming the lid down. "We'll have to tow her back to Birmingham."

Omak leaned into the buggy and brought his rucksack out. "At least the virus is still here."

"Get rid of it," Silva said.

"Not just yet," Omak said, holding up the test tube to the sunlight. "This may be just what we need." He put the test tube back into its refrigerated flask.

"What are you planning?" Silva asked.

"Wait and see," Omak replied, winking. "Let's get the Blood Bug hitched up, then you can tow me back to the city."

The journey back was bumpy and hot. Omak had to sit in his own car to steer it while Silva pulled it along. The steering felt heavy and Omak didn't like being towed. He liked the freedom of the road and being able to escape from the narrow streets of Birmingham.

At last, the walls of the city came into view and then its big gates. Once they were inside, Omak signalled to Silva to stop. Then he climbed out.

"OK, we need to get to the Mayor's office straight away," Omak said. "If what you're saying is right then he won't expect to see me. So you lead the way."

"What are you going to do?" Silva looked confused.

"Just spring a little surprise on him," Omak said, and he grinned.

Silva shook her head. "I hope you know what you're doing," she said. "Mayor Blanchard's a powerful man. If we get this wrong, it'll be his word against ours."

"Trust me," Omak grinned again.

They parked their cars and hurried to the Mayor's office. Omak swallowed hard. For all his brave words, his stomach felt like a knot had been tied in it and his mind was full of doubts.

What if nobody believed them? What if his plan didn't work and the police just threw them in prison?

There was only one way to find out.

CHAPTER 6

Omak and Silva pushed through the crowds of people towards the Mayor's office. Omak gripped the test tube in his fist. To think the contents of this little glass tube could have turned an entire city into Snappers. He looked around him. *Ordinary people like these*, he thought.

The security guard blocked the door.

"There's a Council session on," he said, when Omak tried to get in. "They can't be disturbed."

"We've got to talk to the Council," Silva pleaded. "It's a matter of life and death!"

The security guard looked harder at Silva. "Don't I know you?"

Omak had an idea. "Yes," he said, his face brightening. "She's Mayor Blanchard's niece. His mother, her grandmother, is dying!"

Silva glanced at Omak and then realised his plan. She sniffed loudly and looked wide-eyed at the security guard. The guard hesitated, glancing from Omak to Silva. He couldn't leave his post but it was clear he believed them.

"OK, then," he said and stood aside. He pointed up the corridor. "The Assembly Room is right at the end there."

Omak and Silva barged past the guard and hurried towards the chamber.

"You go in first and tell them what you know," Omak said. "Then I'll come in and see if we can take Blanchard by surprise!"

Silva nodded and pushed the oak-panelled door wide open. Omak pressed himself against the wall to the side of the big door. He glimpsed a shady room with more oak panels. Tables lined the edge of the room and the Councillors of the city sat around them in a meeting.

"Ladies and gentlemen of the Council," Silva said. "Forgive me for interrupting your important meeting but something terrible has happened."

Omak listened to the cries of alarm and then Blanchard's voice rang out. "What's going on here? Who allowed this Postie to burst into the Council chamber? Guards!"

"I have proof that Mayor Blanchard has been plotting to contaminate the city of London with a powerful Snapper virus!"

Again Omak heard a gasp from the Council.

"That's a very serious allegation, missy," Blanchard spat. "I think you've been out in the sun too long!"

"It's true," Omak cried, leaping into the room with the test tube in his hand. "I have the virus here!" He marched straight towards Blanchard who went pale at the sight of Omak.

"I d-don't know what you're talking about," Blanchard stammered. A bead of sweat trickled down his brow and he licked his lips.

"You told me this was a perfectly safe antidote to Snapper virus," Omak said, striding forwards. "You sent me to London to give it to their medics."

Omak stared at the Councillors sitting around him. They looked confused, then their gazes shifted to Blanchard.

"You're lying!" Blanchard said, but his voice sounded faint and he glanced around the room.

"Then I'll be fine smashing this test tube right here, then," Omak said raising his fist.

"Wait!" Blanchard screamed, reaching out.

Omak pulled the test tube out of reach. Blanchard's shoulders slumped. "OK," he said, "it's true. I planned to wipe out London." He looked up and scanned the Council members. "But it was to help us, don't you see? There are too many people. Not enough food or water. Sooner or later, we're going to have to make harsh choices about who lives and who dies. I did it for our people!" He turned to the man sitting close by. "Councillor Lewis, you understand, don't you?"

Lewis was an older man with grey hair and half-moon glasses perched on his nose. He stood up. "Blanchard, you're a monster," he said. "But we'll see that you get a fair trial. Guards!"

The security guard came thundering through the door, his Taser at the ready. He looked at Silva and then at Omak in confusion.

"Arrest Mayor Blanchard!" the older man said.

But a loud metallic click brought them all to a full stop. Blanchard held a pistol and pointed it at Councillor Lewis. "Don't anybody move," Blanchard said. His hand trembled and he stared wildly at the people in the room. "I only ever wanted what was best for the city. But you can't see that." He began edging around the room towards the door as he spoke. "We sit here, day-in, day-out, arguing over damage to the wall and who is going to repair it, trying to share our shrinking water supply. I could have solved our problems in an instant. But no…"

Blanchard snatched the test tube from Omak. He reached the door and dived out of it before the guard could fire his Taser. Omak hurried after him, followed by Silva.

The sun outside dazzled Omak and at first he couldn't see where Blanchard had gone. Then he heard a gunshot. Across the road, a policeman lay groaning on the ground. Blanchard climbed into the police car and revved away.

"We can use Blue Flash to catch him," Silva shouted. "Come on!"

They hurried to Silva's buggy and climbed in. People dived out of the way and yelled after them as Silva zoomed along the streets towards the main gate. "He must be trying to get out," she said.

"There he is!" Omak yelled. Blanchard had the lights of the police car flashing and was heading for the gates which had been automatically opened at the sound of his sirens.

"Looks like he's heading north!" Silva said, slamming her foot on the accelerator. Omak grinned as they gained on the clumsy police car. It was built more for carrying policemen and prisoners around town, and was quite heavily armoured too. Blue Flash was armour-plated but much lighter and faster.

"We're catching up with him!" Omak said. Then he gave a gasp.

Blanchard had spun the car around and was heading back towards them as fast as he could.

Silva narrowed her eyes and pushed Blue Flash faster. "We'll see who's chicken!" she growled.

"Silva, no!" Omak yelled. "That police car is bigger and heavier. It'll demolish us!"

The police car grew nearer, filling their view. Omak could see Blanchard's mad, staring eyes, his insane grin. At the last second, Silva threw the buggy to one side. Blue Flash rolled once and then landed back on its wheels. Omak put his hand to the strong safety harness as if to thank it for keeping him safe. They sat, dazed, for a second. Blanchard lost control of the police car and it went crashing off the road and into the desert.

"He's getting away!" Silva tried to start the engine but it just spluttered and coughed. Blanchard's police car was shrinking into the distance.

"Come on!" Silva cried, trying the engine again. This time the engine backfired and then roared into life. "Good girl!" Silva slapped the dashboard and put her foot down.

They screamed across the rough desert after Blanchard. The police car was a distant speck kicking up a plume of dust.

"We'll never catch him," Omak groaned.

"Wait a minute," Silva said. "Look. He's stopped."

The car had come to a halt. Silva drove carefully towards it. "It might be some new kind of trick," she said. But Omak wasn't sure.

They came to the car, its lights still flashing, but it was empty. Where was Blanchard? Omak put his breathing mask on and climbed out of Blue Flash, Silva's axe in his hand.

"Where's he gone?" Silva called from the buggy.

"I think I know," Omak said, peering inside. The test tube lay broken on the floor of the vehicle. Some way off, a Snapper was staggering around on its own. "Let's go and see," Omak said.

By the look of him, Mayor Blanchard had got the full dose from the test tube. His face was grey and boils and blisters studded his cheeks and forehead. His hands hung loose at his sides and he stopped when Silva and Omak drove past him. He watched them with his head tilted to one side as their car circled him.

"That's horrible," Silva gasped.

"He got a taste of his own medicine," Omak said. "The test tube must have broken when he nearly hit us and went off the road."

"We can't just leave him," Silva said.

"Why not? It's what he would have done to thousands of people, women and children too," Omak said. "We can't take him back. I reckon it serves him right."

Mayor Blanchard watched, his face blank, as Blue Flash vanished into the distance. He couldn't remember who he was, all he knew was hunger. He was so hungry it hurt. He stumbled off in search of meat.

Omak and Silva went back to the police car and set fire to it. "That should destroy what's left of the virus," said Silva, watching the flames and the thick black smoke. "What will you do now?"

Omak shrugged. "I don't know. I was hoping this mission would pay off all Mum's debts," he said. "I'm still broke and now I need to get my car fixed too. I'm worse off than before."

"We could work together for a while," Silva said, flashing Omak a smile. "I think we make a pretty neat team. I'll share my wages until you get your car fixed."

"You'd do that for me?" asked Omak, staring at Silva.

"Yeah, I often need a partner on my missions," she said. "You can handle yourself and you're pretty good company. What do you say?"

Omak could feel himself blushing. "Sure," he said. "Why not? Thanks… partner!"

Silva grinned and fist-bumped Omak. "Let's get back to the city, then. We've got work to do!"

THE END